ZANE:
NINJA OF ICE

By Greg Farshtey

SCHOLASTIC INC.
New York Toronto London Auckland
Sydney Mexico City New Delhi Hong Kong

ISBN 978-0-545-34828-7

20 19 18 17 16 15   14 15 16/0

Printed in the U.S.A.   40
First printing, August 2011

CONTENTS

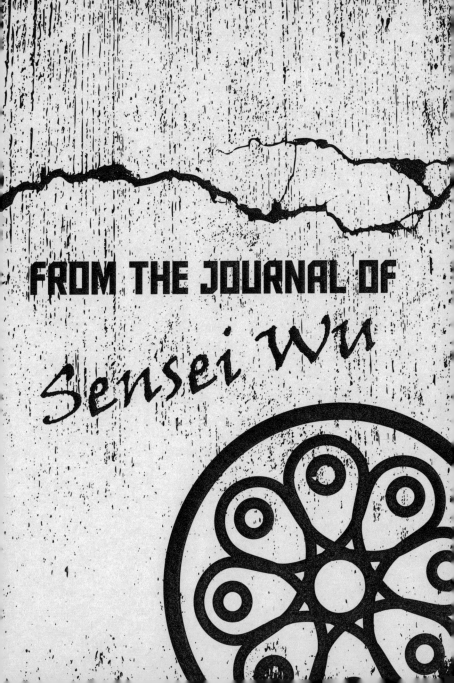

FROM THE JOURNAL OF

Sensei Wu

h, Zane . . . will I ever solve the mystery that surrounds him? More important, will he ever learn the answers to all his questions? Sometimes, I fear not.

I had first heard rumors some time ago about a youth in a northern province capable of withstanding extreme cold. At the time, my other duties kept me from seeking him out. When my brother, Garmadon, threatened to steal the Four Weapons of Spinjitzu, I was forced to seek out potential ninja. This caused my path to finally cross that of Zane.

I found him in a most unusual place. He was sitting at the bottom of an icy lake, meditating. On the shore, a crowd of villagers had gathered, all of them marveling at how long Zane had managed to stay underwater. Anyone else would surely have surfaced after a few minutes due to lack of air or the freezing cold, but Zane seemed to be hardly bothered by either condition. He was, however, quite shocked to open his eyes and see me seated down there with him.

Zane was an orphan . . . or, rather, he thought he might be but was not sure. As it turned out, he was a young man without a past. He said he had awakened one day near his village with no memory of how he had gotten there or where he had been before. All he knew was his name. He made his way into the village and earned a living doing jobs for various people. The fact that Zane was able to do work outdoors in brutally cold conditions

made him much valued, especially by those who preferred to stay indoors by the fire during snowstorms.

When I asked him about training to be a ninja, he was slow to say yes at first. As we talked, he realized that there were many secrets he could uncover through this training. That was how I discovered that Zane loves to learn and is always trying to find out new things.

Zane is, in fact, possibly the smartest of my four ninja. That is, if you measure how smart someone is only by what they have learned from books. Zane can tell you why the grass is green, how a flower grows, what makes a babbling brook sound the way it does. But I have never known him to lie in the grass and look at the clouds, smell a flower, or relax by a brook. I have seen him study the structure of a snowflake, but I wonder if he sees the beauty in the fact that no two are alike?

My other ninja — Jay, Cole, and Kai — have certainly noticed that Zane is a bit different from them. They talk about how he has no sense of humor. He rarely smiles and never laughs and doesn't seem to even get the jokes the other young men tell. Although they like him and respect him, it is sometimes hard for them to feel close to Zane. There is something about him that just feels . . . unique, and no one can identify what it is.

Despite his dedication to his training and the mission, I know Zane is troubled by the questions about his past. He wants to know the answers, but perhaps he fears them as well. What if his parents are still alive and searching for him? Or what if they are bandits and would want him to use his skills for crime? What if the story of his early years holds the key to everything about him that seems so strange to others?

Still, he has shown me again and again that he was the right choice to be my Ninja of Ice. When he faces an enemy, he seeks out points of weakness and targets them. When he strikes, it is not out of anger or fear. Even when faced with a mighty Ice Dragon, Zane does not panic. I have seen Kai let his love for his sister blind him to danger, and Jay's humor desert him in a moment of crisis. But Zane is ice.

What does the future hold for this most mysterious of ninja? I do not know. I believe he hopes his adventures with Kai and the others will somehow lead him to answers about his past. I truly believe he would go to the ends of the world to find out who he really is — and I and my ninja will stand beside him as he searches for clues to this greatest of mysteries.

Zane picked his way carefully down the rocky hillside. His eyes had already adjusted to the darkness, but it would still have been easy to trip and fall. If he were to tumble and cry out, he might be warning Samukai's skeleton warriors that the ninja were nearby. Worse, if he was badly injured, Sensei Wu and Zane's three friends would have to leave him behind. The mission they were on was too dangerous and too important to risk its success.

The "mission" Zane was undertaking at the moment seemed far less important.

Sensei Wu had sent him off to gather sticks so a fire could be built. Although it was a cold evening in the mountains, Zane didn't see the sense in making a campfire. They were very close to the Caves of Despair, the place Sensei was sure would be teeming with skeleton warriors. Why build a fire and potentially give away their position? Not for the first time, Zane wondered if the sensei truly knew what he was doing.

The hillside suddenly grew much steeper. Zane found himself running faster than he wanted to toward the bottom, and only reaching out for a nearby tree slowed him. He glanced up and noted there were a number of branches that would make good firewood. As silently as possible, he began to climb the tree.

There could, of course, have been another good reason why the sensei sent him off on this task. He had been traveling with the other ninja—Cole, Jay, and Kai—for days

now, but he did not really fit in with them. Despite the danger they all were facing, the three youths were always **laughing and joking**. Zane never joined in. In fact, he couldn't remember ever really doing that. He had always been a serious person, devoted to meditation, and hadn't had time for humor and games.

The others didn't know that about him. All they saw was someone who didn't "get" the joke. Maybe they were beginning to wonder if Zane was afraid of the challenges ahead of them, and that was why he was so grim. If they had doubts about him, it might cause problems in battle. Maybe the sensei wanted time alone with the three to discuss this, so he sent Zane off on a pointless job.

Zane didn't think he was afraid. He certainly respected the power of Garmadon and Samukai; only a fool would not. But the feelings that came with fear—cold sweat, trembling, heart pounding—were absent

from him. Much of what the ninja would face was still unknown, and Zane saw no point in fearing the unknown. It was a waste of energy.

He was about to break off a small branch when he heard a twig **snap** down below. Flattening himself against the tree trunk, he waited and watched. In a few moments, he saw the moonlight gleaming off the polished bones of a skeleton warrior. The skeleton was alone and muttering to himself as he walked.

"'Go get the wood, Nuckal,'" grumbled the skeleton. "'Pick up those rocks, Nuckal.' 'Stop eating all the donuts, Nuckal.' Orders, orders, orders, that's all I ever hear."

Zane knew what he had to do. This Nuckal might stumble upon the camp and see Sensei Wu and the others. He would then rush back and report to Samukai. If the skeletons found out about the ninja now, it would be a disaster. The success of the mission depended on surprise.

He waited until Nuckal was right under the tree. Then Zane let go of the trunk and jumped down on top of the skeleton. Nuckal let out an **"OOF"** as Zane landed on him, and the two rolled around on the ground until they smacked into a big rock. Zane was stunned for an instant, allowing the skeleton to get to his bony feet.

"Ha!" said Nuckal. "You're my prisoner!"

Zane rolled aside and sprang into a crouch, a shuriken in his hand. "No. You are my prisoner."

"I said it first," insisted Nuckal.

"I hardly think that matters," Zane answered. "I have a shuriken. You dropped your sword fifteen-point-two feet up the hill. How can I be your prisoner if you have no weapon?"

Nuckal smiled and tapped his head with a long finger of bone. "I have my brain . . . well, actually, I don't really, but I'll bet I'm still smarter than you."

"Why would you think that?" asked Zane.

"For one thing, when I climb trees, I don't fall out of them," Nuckal said, with pride in his voice. "And I don't **run around in the dark** by myself in the middle of the night where I might run into trouble."

"Actually, I am pretty sure that is what you were doing when we met," Zane replied.

"Shows what you know," snapped Nuckal. "When you work for Samukai, you're never alone. Someone is always watching you to make sure you don't eat all the donuts."

Zane frowned. "How can you eat donuts when you have no stomach?"

Nuckal started to answer, then paused, looking confused. A moment later, he opened his mouth again to speak, and stopped again, seeming even more puzzled than before. He looked down at the ground and scratched his skull. Finally, he glared at Zane and said, "That's none of your business!"

"Turn around," said Zane. "I am taking you back to my friends."

Nuckal shook his head. "*You* turn around. Samukai will want to talk to you."

Zane threw his shuriken. It glanced off Nuckal's skull and into the woods. The skeleton **staggered** for a second, but his bone was like armor so he wasn't harmed. Then the two began to fight furiously. First one was winning, then the other, but they were too evenly matched for either to win. They were rolling around on the grass when Nuckal hit his head on a rock and stopped fighting, dazed.

Zane got to his feet. *If I knew Spinjitzu, I could win, but I don't yet. We could fight all night, and if I lost, it would put the others in danger. Still, he's not too bright, so maybe . . .*

"You can't capture me," Zane said suddenly. **"I'm not really here."**

"Huh?" said Nuckal. "But you fell out of a tree and now you're standing right there."

"A tree?" Zane said in disbelief. "Did you ever hear of a ninja falling out of a tree before?"

"Well . . . no," Nuckal admitted.

"Then it doesn't make sense that one did tonight," said Zane. "Want to know what really happened?"

Nuckal nodded. Zane couldn't tell if the skeleton was genuinely starting to disbelieve his own eyes or just waiting to see how far the ninja would push this, but he pressed on anyway.

"You were in your camp," said Zane. "Someone told you to go out and look for wood."

"Sure, Kruncha did," said Nuckal.

"Just before you left, Kruncha told you a joke," said Zane. "Ummmm . . . how did the ninja get up in the tree?"

Nuckal brightened. "I don't know, how?"

"He hid inside an acorn and let a squirrel carry him up," said Zane, doing his best to sound the way Jay did when he told a joke.

Nuckal laughed. "**Ha!** An acorn! Some big ninja hiding inside a little acorn . . . that's a good one."

Zane took a step backward. "Right. In fact, you were thinking about that joke the whole time you were walking here."

"I was?"

Zane took another step back. "Sure. Think about it—a little squirrel carrying a ninja up a tree. That's funny."

The ninja wasn't really sure if it was funny or not, but he had heard Cole tell the joke once and the others had laughed. Nuckal certainly seemed to like it, as he started laughing even harder this time.

"So there you were, minding your own business, thinking about the joke, when you tripped and hit your, um, skull on a rock," Zane continued. "Naturally, you got all

confused. When you got up, you thought you really were seeing a ninja who had been up in a tree. But, of course, you weren't."

"Right," said Nuckal. "Of course. That would be ridiculous. **A ninja up a tree?** You would have to be really stupid to believe that."

Zane took another step back. He was almost completely hidden by darkness now. "One more thing: I wouldn't tell anyone back at your camp about what you thought you saw. They wouldn't understand."

"Yeah, they wouldn't . . . ," Nuckal began. But the ninja he had been talking to—well, the one he imagined he had been talking to—was gone.

Shrugging, the skeleton turned around and started picking up sticks to bring back to camp. It had certainly been a strange night, but he was glad that the imaginary ninja had been nice enough to admit he wasn't real. It would have been embarrassing to tell

Kruncha he had seen someone who clearly wasn't there.

Zane had gathered an armful of wood and was on his way back to camp. No doubt the others would be waiting for him. He looked forward to telling them about his adventure . . . and that, maybe, he finally got the joke.

CHAPTER 1

Zane sat at the bottom of a half-frozen pond, eyes closed, meditating. The water was so bitterly cold that the average person would have been shocked into unconsciousness by exposure to it, but Zane was not bothered at all. He had taught himself how to put the sensation of cold out of his mind, just as he mastered how to slow his breathing. This allowed him to stay underwater for an extraordinary length of time.

The last chance he'd had to meditate this way had been in his village. He had been at the bottom of an icy lake then, when he

25

opened his eyes to see the amazing sight of Sensei Wu, teacup in hand, down there with him. That was when the sensei recruited him to join his team of ninja. Their mission was to stop the evil Lord Garmadon from getting his hands on the Four Weapons of Spinjitzu. So far, they had retrieved two of the four artifacts.

Now, as he pondered in the frigid water, Zane wondered if he had made the right choice in joining Wu's team. True, what they were doing was vitally important to the safety of the world of Ninjago. But Zane had joined for other reasons besides fighting for justice. He had hoped that the chance to travel the world would lead him to answers about his past.

Thus far, that effort had produced no results, and the fact gnawed at him. The frustration he felt at the thought of his failure actually broke his concentration. Suddenly, his lungs were **burning**. He had to

rush to the surface and get a breath of air. Clawing his way back onto shore, he inhaled deeply.

Zane looked around. He was alone. But that was not unusual. In a sense, he was alone wherever he went — for without memories, what does a man have? Zane had awakened one day on a road outside a small village, with no idea how he had gotten there or where he was. He knew his name and little else. The people of the village had taken him in and there he had stayed until Sensei Wu's arrival. Since then, he had been haunted by questions: Who was he? Where had he come from? The answers remained elusive.

Not long ago, he and his friend Kai had traveled back to that village in search of clues to Zane's past. Instead of finding any answers, they found themselves in the middle of a plot by Samukai, ruler of the Underworld, and his skeleton warriors. The two ninja had

smashed the plan, but found nothing to fill in the gaps in Zane's memories.

Zane stood up. There was no point in regrets, he decided. A commitment had been made to Sensei Wu and he had to live up to it. Perhaps when Ninjago was safe from Garmadon, there would be time to resume his search for his past.

Zane was about to leave the pond and head back to camp when he heard a noise nearby. It sounded like a low moan, as if someone were in pain. Zane stopped and listened intently. Yes, it was coming from a cave nearby. The ninja sprinted off in the direction of the sound.

CHAPTER 2

The cave mouth was small and narrow. Zane noted that if the cave itself was the same size, there would be little room to maneuver in a fight. In a split second, he ran down a list of what might be causing the noise. Someone might have been hurt by an animal inside the cave; someone might have been exploring the cave and been injured; the noise might be coming from a wounded animal of some sort; the sound might even be caused by the wind blowing through a gap in the rock somewhere.

Naturally, there was one other possibility:

It was a trap. Samukai had already tried tricking Zane and Kai to get what he thought was a treasure. He might try it again.

Zane stood at the edge of the cave entrance and called out, "**Is some-one in there?** Are you hurt?"

Silence was the only answer.

A voice came from the darkness of the cave. "Help me. . . ." It was a man's voice, faint, as if the person it belonged to was very weak or badly hurt.

Zane didn't hesitate. There was no time to go for help. If someone was injured, he had to aid them, even if it meant risking an ambush. Now with the power of Spinjitzu at his command, he figured the odds were on his side even if it was a trap.

He took a few cautious steps inside, allowing his eyes to adjust to the darkness. The sounds had stopped. Zane peered into the cave, hoping to spot whoever had been calling for help. He saw no one.

"You won't find me here," the voice said, stronger now. "But I do require your help."

Zane looked around, his hands already curling into fists. "Where are you? **Show yourself**."

"The answer to the first is the reason I cannot do the second," the voice replied. "I cannot come to you, Zane. You must come to me."

"Thanks," said Zane, turning around. "I'll pass. Somehow, I have the feeling the cost of helping you would be a little too high."

The ninja intended to head for the exit, but there was nothing there but darkness now. He couldn't see a way out. Still, he did not panic. That wasn't Zane's way. If this was an elaborate trap—and maybe even his last battle—he would still face it calmly. As Sensei Wu always said, an angry fighter has already lost the war.

"I am afraid I cannot let you leave until you have heard me out," the voice said gently.

"All I ask is that you listen. No harm will come to you, Zane. If I wanted you dead . . . well, you would be begging for death by now."

Zane turned back toward the direction from which the voice was coming. "Since I don't seem to be going anywhere, say what you have to say. Start with who you are."

A soft chuckle filled the cave. "Don't you know?"

Then the laughter was drowned out by the sound of rock scraping against rock. A crack of light appeared on the cavern floor in front of Zane, growing wider and wider as he watched. When the noise finally stopped, a portion of the stone floor had slid away to reveal a winding staircase.

"I am the stuff of your **night-mares**," said the voice. "I am the bogeyman in all of Sensei Wu's bedtime stories. I am the exile, the outcast, the villain that every tale must have . . . I am Garmadon."

CHAPTER 3

s Zane climbed down the stairs, he did his best to convince himself it was a wise thing to do. If he could confront Garmadon, he reasoned, perhaps he could learn something of the evil one's plans. Then all he would have to do is escape and inform Sensei Wu of what he had learned.

Of course, a little voice in his head said. *People escape from the Underworld every day. Piece of cake.*

There was a sudden hiss of air off to his left. Instinctively, Zane ducked. A half dozen stone daggers flew by overhead, smashing

into the opposite wall. The ninja barely had time to recover when the stairs beneath him flattened into a slide. He tumbled end over end for about one hundred yards before landing hard on a smooth platform of rock.

Zane struggled to his feet. There was darkness all around. He peered over the edges of the platform, but saw nothing. Had he skidded a little more upon landing, he would have gone over the edge and fallen to his death.

"What happened to 'no harm will come to you'?" Zane snapped. "That looks like a lot of potential harm to me."

"I had to be sure you are truly Zane, Ninja of Ice," Garmadon answered. "After all, someone might have created a . . . fake."

"For what purpose?"

"Who knows?" said Garmadon. "Why do people hide Golden Weapons that might otherwise benefit humanity? I long ago gave

up trying to determine the motivations of others."

The platform began to descend. Zane noticed the temperature falling, not nearly enough to be uncomfortable yet, but it was definitely getting colder.

"How far down am I going?" he asked.

"If it's up to me," answered Garmadon, "**all the way**."

The platform finally came to a stop after what felt like a very long time. The temperature was easily below zero here, and Zane doubted this was the lowest level of the Underworld. *So I still have something to look forward to,* he thought.

It was dark, darker than any place Zane had been. Shadows skittered along the walls, moving like rodents but much too large to be any rat Zane had ever seen. Other than his own breathing, there was no sound. That was perhaps the biggest surprise. Zane had expected to hear the sound of marching **skeleton warriors**.

"I gave them the day off," Garmadon answered, as if he had read the ninja's mind. "I wanted us to have time to talk."

"About what?"

"About you."

"Thanks," said Zane curtly. "But I'm shy. I prefer not to talk about myself."

"Then I will carry the conversation," said Garmadon. "We can talk about your skill as a ninja . . . your mission . . . your new friends . . . or perhaps you would rather talk about . . . your parents?"

CHAPTER 4

Zane's eyes narrowed. "My parents? What trick are you trying to pull?"

"No trick," Garmadon replied. "Come now, Zane, I have been trapped down here for . . . oh, a long time now. It is not, as you can see, a place bursting at the seams with entertainment opportunities. What else is there to do but observe the surface world? I have followed the course of many, many lives up there over the centuries, yours included."

Zane was intrigued. He hated feeling that way—he knew this had to be some ploy of Garmadon's—but he couldn't help wanting to

hear more. "So you're saying—" he began.

"That I know all about your past," Garmadon said. "Who you are, where you come from, why you left . . . I have all the answers, and they are yours for the asking."

"I . . . see," said Zane. "You're being very generous."

Garmadon laughed. It was a foul sound. "I don't believe I know that word. Of course, I want something in return. I am going to escape this place, Zane, no matter how my hated brother may try to prevent it. When I do, I will need warriors by my side— *competent* warriors, not Samukai's bumblers. I want you, Zane, to lead my ninja."

"Your ninja?" asked Zane. "What ninja?"

The terrible answer came in an instant. Shadows detached themselves from the walls, shadows in the shape of **ninja warriors**. As they advanced on Zane, he could see that each carried a sword of pure darkness. Soon he was

surrounded by at least a dozen spectral fighters.

Zane braced himself for a fight, at the same time reaching down into himself to find a center of inner calm. There was no room for fear in the upcoming struggle. He had to analyze his opponents rationally and find their weaknesses.

The first few shadow ninja moved in. Zane immediately saw that their fighting styles were clumsy imitations of Kai and Jay. Their blows had power behind them, but no artistry. Zane parried them easily. More joined the fight, this time imitating the moves of Cole, the ninja team leader. Again, Zane easily fended them off, though the sheer number of opponents was beginning to tax him.

The last group charged now. These were shadowy versions of Sensei Wu himself, and they were far better fighters. For the first time, Zane had to put real effort into protecting himself, which left him wide open to blows

from the other shadows. Too much more of this, and he would go down in defeat.

The time had come. Drawing on all his willpower, Zane began to spin in place. Soon, he was a **whirlwind**, unleashing the power of Spinjitzu against his foes. The shadows did not fall before his attack. Rather, Zane's cyclone shattered them into fragments of darkness that flew around the chamber.

When the last of the enemies had vanished, Zane slowed down and came to a halt. He had won. But was the battle over, or would Garmadon now unleash more ninja on him? There were plenty of shadows here to draw them from. Zane had a realistic sense of his own abilities. He knew he could not survive too many more fights like that.

"As you can see," said Garmadon, "my ninja need a little work."

"It seems they'll do, for now," said Zane,

trying to catch his breath. "But it's lucky for you Kai isn't here."

"So you can see why I need a youth of your skill to train and lead my warriors," said Garmadon. "And in exchange, you get the answers to every question that has plagued you — a more than fair trade, in my opinion."

"Speaking of opinions," Zane laughed, "yours must not be very high of me, if you think I would ever accept such an offer. I know all about you, Garmadon — your ambition, your hunger for power, your plans to dominate Ninjago. I would *never* help you. **Never.**"

Garmadon's voice grew very low, its tone betraying the anger he felt at Zane's words. "You know only what my brother wishes for you to know. As someone or other once said, 'my enemy has written all the books.'"

"Meaning?"

"Meaning there are two sides to every

story," Garmadon replied. "Do you have the courage to hear mine?"

Zane didn't know what to say. He didn't trust Garmadon at all. Sensei Wu had told him and the others more than once what a liar his brother could be. Yet part of the quest for justice was learning all the facts about a situation, rather than allowing your own prejudices to determine your actions. Could he truly be sure there was no more to the story of Wu and Garmadon than what he had been told?

"Go ahead," Zane said finally. "Tell your tale."

CHAPTER 5

The air in front of Zane began to whirl. Colors bled into one another in a giant kaleidoscope, and then a picture began to form in midair. Zane saw a much younger Sensei Wu and someone he assumed was Garmadon. There was a tall, shadowy figure standing before the brothers. Zane got an unmistakable sense that this was a man of power.

"My father," said Garmadon softly. "He created this world, did you know that? I never understood why. With two sons to look after, he chose to take on the responsibility of millions more. I suppose whatever need he

had for . . . respect? worship? . . . wasn't fully satisfied by Wu and me."

Now the figure was lifting a cloth from a table to reveal the Four Weapons of Spinjitzu. The Scythe of Quakes, Nunchuks of Lightning, Dragon Sword of Fire, and Shurikens of Ice were incredibly **powerful artifacts**. It was said that their energies were so great that no one could control all four at once. It was to protect these Weapons from Garmadon that Sensei Wu had assembled Zane and his fellow ninja. Up to now, they had been in a race against the skeleton warriors with whom Garmadon was allied to retrieve the Weapons and keep them safe.

"My father's gift to the two of us," said Garmadon. "Amazing workmanship, wouldn't you agree? He told us that when he died, the responsibility for their safekeeping would be up to us. Nothing like having something to look forward to, hmmm?"

The scene shifted again. Garmadon's father was gone now, but the Weapons remained. Sensei Wu and Garmadon were preparing them for transport.

"Sending the Weapons off to a place of concealment was actually Wu's idea," said Garmadon. "He always did like playing **hide-and-seek**, even as a child. Of course, I always won. I found it quite simple, really."

"You excel at finding things?" asked Zane.

"Oh, no," Garmadon laughed. "I excel at manipulating my brother. You see, he would hide. I would seek. After a short time, I would grow bored with trying to find him. So I would begin to sound panicked, as if I were afraid something might have happened to him. It was no longer about the game . . . it was now about Wu's safety, you see. My tenderhearted brother would feel guilty that I was so worried and would reveal himself . . . and so I won again."

"I think he knows you a little better now," said Zane.

"He certainly thinks he does," Garmadon countered. "But millennia trapped in the Underworld can change a person. Wu really has no idea what I am capable of . . . **do you**?"

"I am sure I will find out," Zane replied, "if you do not bore me to death first."

The colors swirled once more and now Zane was seeing Garmadon attempting to steal the Golden Weapons. Wu suddenly appeared, pointing an accusing finger at his brother. The image froze on that moment.

"And there we have it," said Garmadon. "That was the turning point. That is the single moment that defines me in my brother's eyes. Anything and everything else we had shared in the past was **forgotten** right then."

"You were trying to steal the Weapons!" Zane said, his voice echoing off unseen walls. "Of course Sensei Wu turned on you. What did you think he would do?"

"Honestly?" Garmadon answered. "I thought he was asleep. I thought I would be long gone with the Four Weapons before he ever realized they were missing. And then we would play hide-and-seek again . . . by my rules."

"But it didn't work out that way," said Zane. As he talked, his eyes darted about, looking for something that might be a control panel for the platform. It was all very interesting hearing about Garmadon's youth, but there was still the little matter of escaping from this place to think about. Unfortunately, he couldn't see anything but shadows and stone.

"No. It did not, much to the misfortune of Ninjago," said Garmadon. "Think about it, Zane. Those Weapons could have been — and still might be — used to vanquish terrible evils that plague your planet. Instead, Wu chose to hide them away. When I wanted to put them to use, I was condemned as

evil and **banished** here."

"You wanted to use them for conquest and destruction," spat Zane.

"According to Wu," Garmadon shot back. "Suppose, just suppose, he has a reason to not be completely honest with you and your friends. Suppose, for all his sterling reputation, my brother is afraid to use those Weapons? That is the truth. He is afraid to do what is necessary to protect this world from evil."

Zane was not known for his sense of humor, but even he almost laughed at that. Sensei Wu had devoted his entire life to battling the forces of darkness. Now Garmadon—a shadow allied with an army of skeletons—was trying to act as if he were the true crusader for justice.

"Whose life have the Weapons improved? No one's," Garmadon continued. "What villain have they defeated? What problem have they solved? None. They have been hidden away, gathering dust, of use to no one. Is that

why they were created? I say **no**."

Zane had had enough. "And who is the judge of how they should be used? You? Samukai? One of the skeleton warriors who attacked my village?"

This time, the answer did not come from Garmadon. Instead, the scene shifted to show a kindly-looking man with a little boy sitting on his lap. The man was saying, "When you grow up, you will be very wise and very strong. I am sure of it. You must always remember that your wisdom and strength—indeed, any power you may someday have—should be used for good. To do any less would be to prove yourself unworthy of that power, Zane."

Suddenly Zane, the Ninja of Ice, who could meditate in a freezing lake without discomfort—felt terribly cold. "Who—who is that?"

"I promised you information—consider this a sign of my good faith," Garmadon answered. "That, Zane, is your father."

Zane stood and stared for a very long time. It had to be true. The boy did look like him, and he could see an aged version of his own features on the face of his . . . father?

Father.

The word sounded strange, even rolling around in his brain. He knew it would sound even stranger if he tried to say it out loud. He reached out to touch the image, but his hand passed right through it as if it were a ghost.

"My . . ." Zane couldn't bring himself to say the word. "This man . . . where is he? Who is he?"

"Ah-ah," said Garmadon. "As I made him appear . . ." The image abruptly vanished. "So can I make him disappear. Consider this a glimpse of the treasure trove of information that waits for you here. All you have to do is say yes."

Zane stared at the empty space where his father's image had been. "Yes . . . to what?"

"Well, I am not asking you stab your friends in the back," Garmadon answered, "though that certainly would be amusing. Just slow them down a bit, here and there. You can manage that. And when the time comes, choose the winning side in the fight."

"You're asking me to be a **traitor**!"

"That's such an ugly word," said Garmadon. "I am asking you to be . . . practical. If the choice is certain victory plus a head full of knowledge about your past or sure death in battle with my skeletons, the realistic man would find the decision an easy one."

Zane shook his head. He was actually

considering Garmadon's offer, and he hated himself for it. Would this be what his father wanted? How could he someday look the man in the face if he had bought the chance to meet him with the lives of his friends?

Yet if he said no, **then what**? He would never find his father, or mother, or home. He would spend the rest of his life an empty shell, without a past. Maybe he could help Garmadon only a little, not enough to really cause a problem, and learn at least some of what he needed to know.

"Three . . . two . . . one," Garmadon counted down. "Time's up."

There was a flash of light. Zane blinked to clear his vision. When he could see, he found himself out of the Underworld. He was back at the edge of the pond. Had it all been a dream? No, it couldn't have been, he decided. He never had dreams like that.

Any doubts were resolved when he saw a shadow shift beneath a tree, and heard

the voice of Garmadon saying, "If we have a bargain, Zane, you will know what to do and when to do it. If you should need more convincing . . ."

The waters of the pond stirred. In their depths, Zane could see his father with an elderly woman. They were sitting in a farmhouse with a picture of Zane on the table before them. The woman—his mother?—was crying softly. Then the image was gone as swiftly as it had appeared.

CHAPTER 7

Zane made his way back to camp. The first person he encountered was Kai.

"Hey, are you all right?" the Ninja of Fire asked. "You look like you've seen a ghost."

"Or two," Zane replied softly.

"Huh?"

"Never mind. Where is Sensei Wu?"

Kai pointed toward the center of camp. Sensei Wu was sitting by the campfire, staring pensively into the flames. Zane walked over and sat down next to him. At first, the sensei did not seem to even notice his presence. But after a few moments, Wu said, "The

birds of worry nest in your hair, Zane. Do you wish to tell me why?"

Zane hesitated. Did he really want to say, *Well, I was considering betraying you for my own selfish reasons?* No, it was best not to.

"No, Sensei," he answered.

Wu nodded. "Do you believe your doubts and fears threaten our mission?"

"I don't know," answered Zane.

The sensei sipped from a cup of tea that seemed to appear as if by magic in his hand. Zane would have sworn it had not been there moments before. "There was once a **golden dragon fish**," the aged warrior began. "It lived among a very great school of its brothers. One day, the fish broke away from the school seeking adventure, and met a shark. The shark invited the little fish to travel with him and feed off the mites that collected on his scales. Soon, the dragon fish fell into the way of life of traveling with the shark. Its

success was linked to that of the great predator.

"Months later, the shark spotted a school of fish and went on the hunt. To his dismay, the dragon fish saw that the prey fish the shark was after were his brothers. He had time to warn them—but doing so would mean the end of his pleasant life with the shark . . . decisions, decisions."

Does he know? wondered Zane. *Or only suspect? I must be careful.*

"Well, questions of loyalty are always difficult ones," said the Ninja of Ice. "It is not always easy to know which side to be on, or what to believe."

"Believe in yourself," the sensei said. "Be true to what you believe, to your ideals, and you will find your choice has been made for you."

"Thank you, Sensei," said Zane. "I believe I understand. By the way . . . what happened to the dragon fish?"

"Oh, he fled the shark and warned his brothers."

"That is commendable," said Zane. "His loyalty to his school was more important to him than his own interests. He must have been very proud of himself for making such a choice."

"Indeed, he was," the sensei replied, "right up to the moment that the shark ate him."

Zane **shuddered**.

Cole approached, carrying the golden Scythe of Quakes, one of the Four Weapons of Spinjitzu. Like Zane, Cole was a pretty serious sort. He took being field leader of the ninja team very seriously. "Are you ready, Zane?" he asked.

"Ready for what?"

"I have not yet told him," Sensei Wu said to Cole. Turning to Zane, he extended his hand. In his palm were the Shurikens of Ice, yet another of the valuable artifacts. "You and Cole have found your Golden Weapons. The

time may come when you are forced to use them. I want you to go some distance from camp and train with them."

"Wait," said Zane, confused. "When we found the Scythe, you told us we must not ever use it. Isn't it dangerous to practice fighting with these Weapons?"

Sensei Wu nodded. "Times change. The wise man changes with them. We have retrieved two of the four Weapons, and my brother, Garmadon, will be growing desperate. **Anything** may happen now."

Zane barely heard his answer. All he could think of was what would happen if he gave the two Golden Weapons to Garmadon. Would that be enough to buy information about his past?

It wouldn't be so bad, would it? he asked himself. *As long as we get the Dragon Sword of Fire and the Nunchuks of Lightning, we can stop Garmadon. It would simply be a stalemate.*

"Let's go," said Cole. "We don't have much time."

"No," Zane replied. "I guess we don't."

Zane took the Shurikens. Something felt wrong about all this, but the image in his mind of his parents drove all other thoughts away. He rose in silence and followed Cole out of the camp.

CHAPTER 8

They stopped walking when they reached an empty area. It wasn't far from the cave where Zane had found Garmadon. If Zane had believed in fate, he would have surely seen this as a sign.

Cole was twirling the Scythe, being careful not to strike anything and unleash the Weapon's seismic power. Soon, he was moving so fast that the Scythe was just a golden blur.

"Get started," Cole ordered. "Try getting the feel of the weight and balance of the Shuriken. That will help you master throwing it."

Zane did as he was told. That feeling that something was wrong kept nagging at him. What was it—something about the Shuriken itself, perhaps? He had held it only briefly when the team had retrieved it from the Ice Fortress. What could have happened between then and now? And was there more to the sensei's decision to allow training with the Golden Weapons than the old man was letting on?

Something whistled through the air past Zane's head. An instant later, Cole hit the ground, unconscious. Zane rushed over to him. He had been struck by a thrown rock. There was a big lump on his head, but the ninja team leader was alive.

A half dozen skeleton warriors stepped out of the surrounding woods, followed by another skeleton, this one with four arms. The Ninja of Ice immediately recognized this new arrival, and knew he was in **serious trouble**.

"Samukai," breathed Zane.

The empty eye sockets of the ruler of the Underworld narrowed. "You flesh-covered types all look alike to me," Samukai rasped. "But I remember you. You're the one with no past. Well, I have news for you: You have no future, either."

Zane glanced from Samukai to Cole, then back again. It was time to make his choice. He took a step away from his fallen friend and raised the Shuriken, as if preparing to throw it. Samukai moved back a little, but none of the other skeletons did. The four-armed warrior knew the legendary power of the Shurikens of Ice: Obviously, his soldiers had no clue what they faced.

A moment passed, then two. Combat or surrender? Loyalty to his team or betrayal on behalf of a life he could not remember? Which would it be? As he turned the Shuriken over and over in his fingers, he felt that sense of wrongness yet again. But this

time he knew its cause . . . and he knew what he had to do.

Zane lowered his arm and extended the Shurikens toward Samukai. "Here. Take them. The Scythe, too — your master knows my price."

Samukai didn't move. His expression was wary. He had not become ruler of the massive Underworld by rushing into traps, and that was what this felt like.

"Who do you think you are trying to deceive, child?" said Samukai. "Some minor shade on his first visit back to Ninjago? One of my idiotic soldiers? Do you expect me to believe you are going to simply hand over two of the Four Weapons of Spinjitzu without a **fight**?"

"Believe it or not," answered Zane. "You have thirty seconds to accept my offer. After that, you can try to take them, but I do not like your chances. Or you can go back to Garmadon and tell him you had the chance

at half of his desired treasure and you turned it down."

Samukai did some quick mental calculations. Garmadon was not his master, despite what this sniveling human thought, but Sensei Wu's dark brother was a powerful ally just the same. It was doubtful Garmadon would take kindly to finding out the Shurikens and Scythe could have been had and were allowed to slip away.

Shoving one of his skeleton warriors toward Zane, Samukai said, "Give the Weapons to this one. He is too slow to know what to do with them, so there is no risk of betrayal. You said Garmadon would know your price—I would like to know it, too. I do not like to 'purchase' items without knowing the terms of sale."

The skeleton approached. Zane handed him the Shurikens, then bent down to pick up the Scythe of Quakes. He gave that to the skeleton as well, saying, "Be careful with these. Dropping them would be . . . bad."

"Answer my question!" snapped Samukai.

"That *is* my price," Zane replied, "the answers to questions."

Samukai took the two Golden Weapons from his warrior. A smile appeared like a crack in his skull. "Do you want us to **strike you down** now? You know, so that you can tell Sensei Wu you were attacked, defeated, and the Weapons stolen from you? I am sure we can make your battle damage look most convincing."

"No, thanks," said Zane. "Just give me what I asked for."

Samukai cocked his head and paused, as if listening to something no one else could hear. Then he said, "Garmadon says, return to the cave. You'll get what you need there."

"What about my friend here?"

Samukai shrugged. "If we wanted him dead, we would have thrown a **bigger rock**."

Zane couldn't argue with that logic,

twisted though it might be. He backed away from the skeletons, keeping an eye on them until they had all withdrawn into the woods. Cole was already beginning to stir. Zane turned and headed for the cave, hoping he would make it inside before his friend spotted him. He didn't want Cole placed in any more danger because of him. What he had to do now, he had to do alone.

CHAPTER 9

The cavern was still pitch-black inside, but now the darkness seemed alive with movement. More of Garmadon's shadow ninja, perhaps? Zane stood still, waiting for the platform to descend and take him to the world below. But nothing happened. His host, it seemed, saw no reason to continue the tour of the Underworld.

"An impressive beginning," said Garmadon, his voice slithering out from all corners of the cave. "I chose wisely, I see."

"Not a beginning," Zane corrected, "an

ending. Give me the information you promised and our deal is done."

"Do you think it is that easy?"

Zane stood his ground and said firmly, "I know it is. I have lived with my mysteries for a long time now and could keep doing it, if necessary. You have spent far longer trapped in the Underworld and cannot stand it. Seems to me that you need me more than I need you."

Garmadon gave a soft chuckle. "Very well, then. A bargain is a bargain. Look, Zane."

Once again, the portal appeared in mid-air. This time, Zane saw himself as a small child with his father and mother. Their home was a small shack in what appeared to be a little village. Zane was sitting on the lawn, playing with a stick, while his father chopped wood and his mother hung up washing.

"Your father was a woodworker," Garmadon said. "He carved wood into axe

handles, toys, plates, bowls, utensils, all sorts of boring things like that. Your mother was a seamstress, sewing new clothes and repairing old ones for others. Between the two of them, they made enough money to keep a little food on the table and take care of their young son."

The scene shifted. Now a much older Zane was walking down a road. It must have been just past sunset, for the road was very dark. All at once, a horse-drawn cart came **thundering** around a curve, dangerously fast. It struck Zane a glancing blow and the young man fell unconscious in the road.

"You were on your way to purchase some supplies from a neighboring town," Garmadon continued. "The driver of the cart never even saw you. The next morning, you awoke in the road with no memory of what had happened. End of story."

"What?" said Zane. "What about my parents? Are they still alive? What village are they from?"

"If you want more, you must do more for me," Garmadon replied.

Zane shook his head. "No. Never."

"Then I have half of the Four Weapons, and you have half the story, and that is how it is," said Garmadon. "It cost you the trust of your friends, your honor, and your pride. It cost me . . . hmmm . . . the hour or so I needed to make up that story."

At first, Zane felt like crying out in anger. Everything Garmadon had told him about his past—it had all been a lie. His parents, his home, all of it, nothing more than a trick to get him to betray Sensei Wu. Yet instead of raging at Garmadon, Zane actually smiled.

This seemed to annoy Garmadon. "What are you smiling about?" he demanded.

"Oh, I was just thinking about bargains,"

Zane answered. "You do get what you pay for, don't you? You gave me a phony past . . . and I gave you phony Weapons of Spinjitzu."

"What?!?" roared Garmadon, loud enough to shake the cavern.

"I can't take the credit," Zane explained. "Your brother must have sensed what you were up to. He gave Cole and me fake versions of our Golden Weapons, suspecting they might wind up in your hands. I didn't know, at first. But when I got ready to throw the Shurikens of Ice at Samukai, I realized they were too light. True gold is very heavy, and this felt more like iron, painted gold."

Zane turned and started walking out of the cave. "I am afraid, Garmadon, you traded a lie for a lie. Our business today has ended."

Three skeletons appeared in the mouth of the cave. Behind him, Zane could feel the shadows taking form as ninja. He was surrounded.

"It is ended when I say it is ended,"

Garmadon snarled. "No one makes a fool out of me."

There was a blur of movement at the entrance to the cave. Something **smashed** into the three skeletons, bowling them over. An instant later, Cole stood alone in their place.

"No one has to, Garmadon," Cole said. "You do such a good job of it by yourself."

The shadow ninja charged. Zane dove forward, landing on his hands, and lashed back with both feet. His kicks staggered two of the ninja. Before the rest could close in, he rolled into a somersault and sprang to his feet next to Cole.

"How did you find me?" asked Zane.

"I saw that rock coming a mile away," Cole replied. "It grazed me . . . well, maybe a little more than that . . . but I was awake the whole time. I would have shown up sooner, but I had to see what you would do."

The shadow ninja rushed out of the

cave. This time, their movements were more fluid, their blows harder, and their imitations of the young ninja more accurate. But this time, Zane was not facing them alone. He and Cole worked like a perfect team, ducking and dodging and then **striking hard**. Cole confused a foe by dropping to his back and then landing a kick in the shadow ninja's midsection, sending him flying through the air. Zane saw a shadowy being coming and leaped high, coming down with a two-fisted slam that smashed the dark ninja into the ground.

After a short but furious battle, the shadow ninja started retreating into the cave. Zane started in after them, but was brought up short by Cole. "No, let them go. We need to get back to the sensei."

"But—"

"Come on. It's over, for now. There will be another day, I promise you."

CHAPTER 10

Sensei Wu was waiting when they got back to camp. He motioned for Zane to join him by the fire. "You guessed that the Weapons were fake, and so you gave them to the enemy."

Zane nodded.

"And if you hadn't known they were frauds? Would you still have handed them over to Samukai? You feel you are not sure of the answer to that question, and it bothers you, does it not?"

Again, Zane nodded, his eyes on the ground.

"Fortunately for us both, I do know the answer," Sensei Wu said, smiling. "I may not know your origins, but I am certain of what is in your heart. Just like the dragon fish, when the time came to make a choice, you would do what is right . . . even if it cost you your life. That is why I chose you. That is why you said yes."

"Thank you, Sensei," said Zane quietly. "But I wonder . . . will I ever know about my past? Will I ever meet my parents?"

"I truly hope so," the sensei replied. "And when you do, tell them the tale of this day . . . tell them how you did their memory honor, even when that memory was lost to you."

Cole walked up to the fire. "Sensei, you said we need to get moving. I have the others packed up and ready."

"Yes, indeed," the sensei said, getting to his feet. "We have a third Weapon to find, but it is not a long journey. Just to the edge of the world and

beyond. There are more mysteries to be explored, my young ninja . . . and, perhaps, some answers to be found along the way."